A True Princess

Adapted by Mary Man-Kong
Based on the screenplay by Brian Hohlfeld
Illustrated by Ulkutay Design Group

Special thanks to Diane Reichenberger, Cindy Ledermann, Sarah Lazar, Charnita Belcher, Tanya Mann, Julia Phelps, Nicole Corse, Sharon Woloszyk, Rita Lichtwardt, Carla Alford, Renee Reeser Zelnick, Rob Hudnut, David Wiebe, Shelley Dvi-Vardhana, Gabrielle Miles, Rainmaker Entertainment, and Walter P. Martishius

A Random House PICTUREBACK® Book

Random House 🏠 New York

Published in the United States by Random House Children's Books, a division of Random House LLC, 1745 Broadway,
New York, NY 10019, and in Canada by Random House of Canada Limited, Toronto, Penguin Random House Companies.
No part of this book may be reproduced or copied in any form without permission from the copyright owner.
Pictureback, Random House, and the Random House colophon are registered trademarks of Random House LLC.
ISBN 978-0-385-38431-5 (pbk) — ISBN 978-0-385-38432-2 (ebook)
randomhouse.com/kids   Printed in the United States of America   10 9 8 7 6 5 4

*O*nce there was a pretty princess named Alexa. She was very shy and wanted to spend her time reading books all by herself. One day, Alexa's grandmother gave her a special book. The book was about a magical princess who was very brave. "How cool would it be if I had magic . . . ?" thought Alexa. "Then I could be good at anything!"

Alexa began reading her book in the royal gardens. When she finally looked up, the princess saw a strange and beautiful door—it looked just like the one on the cover of her new book! Alexa opened the door . . .

. . . and found herself in the most amazing place she had ever seen! There were brightly colored trees, floating islands, mermaids, fairies, and adorable baby unicorns everywhere!

Two girls named Romy and Nori bowed before Alexa. They thought she was a magical princess.

"But I don't have any magic," Alexa said. Romy and Nori pointed to Alexa's hair stick. It had transformed into a glittering golden wand with a gem on top! And her clothes had changed into a glamorous gown.

Alexa tried her new wand, and instantly, Nori's dress turned into a sparkling yellow gown!

Romy and Nori hoped that Alexa could help them save the kingdom of Zinnia from its mean ruler. Malucia was a ten-year-old princess who had been born without magical powers, so she was stealing everyone's magic with her scepter. Malucia had even taken Romy's mermaid tail and Nori's fairy wings!

Suddenly, a fairy named Nola appeared, bringing terrible news. Malucia was on her way to capture the Queen Unicorn and steal her magic. With the Queen Unicorn's powerful magic, Malucia would be unstoppable!

Alexa and her friends quickly set out to save the Queen Unicorn. Luckily, they arrived before Malucia and her minions. Alexa couldn't believe her eyes! With a glittering horn and a magnificent, shimmering mane, the unicorn was the most beautiful thing she had ever seen.

Unfortunately, Malucia and her minions followed them and captured all the magical unicorns. "I'm the only one who can have magic!" Malucia cried as she blasted Alexa with her scepter. Alexa's wand cracked, and she quickly hid while Malucia and her minions fled with the unicorns.

It would have been so easy to return to her quiet life as a princess, but Alexa knew she had to help her friends. Suddenly, glittery sparkles appeared and Alexa's wand was magically fixed! "As long as I have my magic, I promise to do everything I can to get your magic and the unicorns back!" Alexa promised Nori and Romy.

The girls rushed to the palace to stop Malucia—but it was too late! The wicked princess was draining all the magic from the Queen Unicorn!

Alexa noticed that Malucia's scepter was starting to crack. That gave the princess an idea. She pretended to surrender to Malucia. "You want all the magic? Take it!" Alexa cried. Malucia cackled and pointed her scepter at Alexa, draining her magical energy.

Malucia's scepter began vibrating and grew brighter and brighter. It had absorbed too much energy. Alexa saw her chance and threw her wand into the scepter's crack. *Kaboom!* The scepter exploded! It sent Malucia flying through the air, and she landed in a huge frosted cake.

Freed from Malucia's scepter, shimmering magic swept through Zinnia and returned to all the mermaids, fairies, and unicorns. Everyone cheered!

"You gave up your magic for us," Nori said to Alexa.

"It was worth it to help my friends," Alexa replied.

Alexa soon said good-bye to her new friends and returned to her own world, feeling confident and assured. No longer shy, she even surprised her parents by attending the royal ball. Alexa danced with her friends, no longer envying the magical princess from her book. She had learned that real magic and happiness come from within.